W9-CFS-385

Library of Congress Cataloging in Publication Data: Kahn, Peggy. The Care Bears' Night Before Christmas. "A Care Bear book from Random House, New York." SUMMARY: An adaptation of "The Night Before Christmas" in which Santa visits the Care Bears, who are nestled on puffy cloud beds. 1. Children's stories, American. [1. Bears—Fiction. 2. Santa Claus—Fiction. 3. Christmas—Fiction. 4. Stories in rhyme] I. Kamm, Diane, ill. II. Moore, Clement Clarke, 1779–1865. Night Before Christmas. III. Title. PZ8.3.K12425Cat 1985 [E] 85-42532 ISBN: 0-394-87502-8 (trade); 0-394-97502-2 (lib. bdg.)

Weekly Reader Children's Book Club presents

The Care Bears' Night Before Christmas

adapted by Peggy Kahn
illustrated by Diane Kamm

A Care Bear™ Book from Random House, New York

'Twas the night before Christmas
And as you can see,
All the Care Bears were just
As excited as me!

Their stockings were hung
In the Hall of the Heart,
And the Bears hoped that Santa
Would soon play his part.

The Care Bears were nestled on puffy cloud beds,
While visions of sugarplums danced in their heads.

And Grams in her bonnet, and we Bears in our caps,

Had just settled down for Christmas Eve naps.

When over our rainbow there arose such a clatter,
I bounced off of my cloud to see what was the matter.

When what to the eyes of this Bear should appear,
But a miniature sleigh and eight tiny reindeer...

With a little old driver—a bright, lively elf—
I knew it must be jolly Santa himself!

More rapid than rockets, his reindeer they came.
And he whistled, and shouted, and called them by name!
"Now, Dasher! Now, Dancer! Now, Prancer and Vixen!
On, Comet! On, Cupid! On, Donder and Blitzen!
Over the rainbow to the Care Bears' great hall!
Now dash away! Dash away! Dash away, all!"

To the Hall of the Heart Santa's reindeer all flew,
With a sleigh full of toys, and Santa Claus, too.
And then, in a twinkling, I heard on the roof
The prancing and pawing of each little hoof.

FOR SANTA

As I floated up, and was turning around,
Down the chimney Santa came with a bound!
He was dressed all in red from his head to his toes,
And a twinkle of stardust hung on his clothes.
A bundle of toys was slung on his back.
He was glad that the Care Bears had left him a snack!

His eyes—how they twinkled, his dimples, how merry!
His cheeks were like roses, his nose like a cherry!
His nice little mouth was drawn up like a bow,
And the beard on his chin was as white as the snow.
He had a broad face and a round little belly
That shook, when he laughed, like a bowl full of jelly.

From deep in his pack he took presents with care
That were sure to delight each and every Care Bear:
A new blanket for Bedtime, a star wand for Wish;
A rod for Good Luck Bear to catch a big fish...
There wasn't a Care Bear whom Santa forgot!
He'd thought about everyone in Care-a-Lot!

He spoke not a word, but went straight to his work.
He filled all the stockings; then turned with a jerk,

And laying his finger to one side of his nose,
And giving a nod, up the chimney he rose!

He whistled a tune as he hopped on his sleigh.
The reindeer sprang up and they all flew away.

"And now down to earth with my bundle of toys.
I've stockings to fill for the girls and the boys!"
Then I heard him say,
As he drove out of sight,
"Merry Christmas, dear Care Bears,
And to you a good night!"